P9-DEE-051

E
HIL

Hillert, Margaret.

The little cowboy and
the big cowboy.

$19.93

DATE			

PLATTEKILL PUBLIC LIBRARY
2047 State Route 32
Modena, NY 12548
845-883-7286
http://plattekill.lib.ny.us

BAKER & TAYLOR

WITHDRAWN

The Little Cowboy and the Big Cowboy

by Margaret Hillert
Illustrated by Dan Siculan

DEAR CAREGIVER, The *Beginning-to-Read* series is a carefully written collection of classic readers you may remember from your own childhood. Each book features text comprised of common sight words to provide your child ample practice reading the words that appear most frequently in written text. The many additional details in the pictures enhance the story and offer the opportunity for you to help your child expand oral language and develop comprehension.

Begin by reading the story to your child, followed by letting him or her read familiar words and soon your child will be able to read the story independently. At each step of the way, be sure to praise your reader's efforts to build his or her confidence as an independent reader. Discuss the pictures and encourage your child to make connections between the story and his or her own life. At the end of the story, you will find reading activities and a word list that will help your child practice and strengthen beginning reading skills.

Above all, the most important part of the reading experience is to have fun and enjoy it!

Shannon Cannon

Shannon Cannon,
Literacy Consultant

Norwood House Press • P.O. Box 316598 • Chicago, Illinois 60631
For more information about Norwood House Press please visit our website at *www.norwoodhousepress.com* or call 866-565-2900.

LIBRARY OF CONGRESS CATALOGING-IN-PUBLICATION DATA

Hillert, Margaret.
  The little cowboy and the big cowboy / Margaret Hillert ; illustrated by Dan Siculan. — Rev. and expanded library ed.
    p. cm. — (Beginning-to-read series)
  Summary: A little cowboy and his father ride horses, round up cattle, mend a fence, practice roping, cook over a campfire, and sleep outdoors in their sleeping bags.
    ISBN-13: 978-1-59953-187-8 (library edition : alk. paper)
    ISBN-10: 1-59953-187-9 (library edition : alk. paper) [1.
  Cowboys—Fiction.] I. Siculan, Dan, ill. II. Title.
  PZ7.H558Lg 2008
  [E]—dc22
                                                    2008001643

Beginning-to-Read series (c) 2009 by Margaret Hillert.
Library edition published by permission of Pearson Education, Inc. in arrangement with Norwood House Press, Inc. All rights reserved.
This book was originally published by Follett Publishing Company in 1981.

Here is a little cowboy.

And here is a big cowboy.

Here is something little
for the little cowboy.
It can go.
It can run.

Here is something big
for the big cowboy.
It can go.
It can run, too.

The two cowboys can ride.
It is fun to ride.
Fun to ride away.

But the two cowboys
have to work, too.
The little cowboy can
help the big cowboy.

Here is something to do.
Look here. Look here.
What do you see?

The big cowboy can get
the big ones.
That is good.

The little cowboy can get
the little ones.
That is good, too.

Oh, look here.
Something is down.
Here is work to do.

Work, work, work.
Make it good.
Now no one can get out.

Here is something that
is fun to do.
The big cowboy can do it.

But the little cowboy
can not do it.
The little cowboy will have
to work at it.

Oh, look at this.
How big it is!
Big, big, big.

And look at this.
Look what the cowboys see now.
How pretty it is.

21

The big cowboy will make
something to eat.
The little cowboy will work, too.

23

24

The big cowboy and the little
cowboy can eat now.
My, this is good.

Here is something cowboys like.
You can play it.
It is fun to play.

The little cowboy can
play a little one.
The big cowboy can
play a big one.

The little cowboy gets
down in here.
And the big cowboy gets
down in here.

The cowboys do not have to
work now.
This is good.
The cowboys like to do this.

The following activities support the findings of the National Reading Panel that determined the most effective components for reading instruction are: Phonemic Awareness, Phonics, Vocabulary, Fluency, and Text Comprehension.

Phonemic Awareness: The diphthong /oi/ sound

Oral Blending: Say the sounds of the following words separately and ask your child to listen to the sounds and say the whole word:

/b/ + /oi/ = boy   /oi/ +/l/ = oil

/b/ + /oi/ + /l/ = boil   /k/ + /oi/ +/ /n = coin

/t/ + /oi/ = toy   /j/ + /oi/ + /n/ = join

/j/ + /oi/ = joy   /f/ + /oi/ + /l/ = foil

/n/ + /oi/ + /z/ = noise

Phonics: The letters o and i

1. Demonstrate how to form the letters **o** and **i** for your child.

2. Have your child practice writing **o** and **i** at least three times each.

3. Write down the following and ask your child to add the letters oi or oy to complete each word:

    b _ _   _ _ l   t _ _   c _ _ n   f _ _ l   j _ _

    n _ _ se   s _ _   s _ _ l   j _ _ n   p _ _ nt   b _ _ l

4. Ask your child to read each word.

Vocabulary: Compound Words

1. Explain to your child that sometimes two words can be put together to make a new word. These are called compound words. The story has two compound words: **cowboy** and **something**.

2. Write down the following words on separate pieces of paper:

sand	air	skate	box	ball
paper	room	butter	news	plane
board	book	back	birth	base
note	bed	day	fly	pack

3. Help your child move the pieces of paper around to form compound words.
   Possible answers: *sandbox, airplane, skateboard, baseball, newspaper, bedroom, backpack, birthday, butterfly, notebook*

Fluency: Echo Reading

1. Reread the story to your child at least two more times while your child tracks the print by running a finger under the words as they are read. Ask your child to read the words he or she knows with you.

2. Reread the story, stopping after each sentence or page to allow your child to read (echo) what you have read. Repeat echo reading and let your child take the lead.

Text Comprehension: Discussion Time

1. Ask your child to retell the sequence of events in the story.

2. To check comprehension, ask your child the following questions:
   - What kinds of work do the cowboys do?
   - What kinds of special clothes do the cowboys wear?
   - Where did the cowboys sleep? Do you think they were scared?
   - If you were a cowboy/cowgirl, what would you like most about it?

WORD LIST

The Little Cowboy and the Big Cowboy **uses the 50 words listed below.** This list can be used to practice reading the words that appear in the text. You may wish to write the words on index cards and use them to help your child build automatic word recognition. Regular practice with these words will enhance your child's fluency in reading connected text.

a	get(s)	make	see
and	go	my	something
at	good		
away		no	that
	have	not	the
big	help	now	this
but	here		to
	how	oh	too
can		one(s)	two
cowboy(s)	in	out	
	is		what
do	it	play	will
down		pretty	work
	like		
eat	little	ride	you
	look	run	
for			
fun			

ABOUT THE AUTHOR Margaret Hillert has written over 80 books for children who are just learning to read. Her books have been translated into many different languages and over a million children throughout the world have read her books. She first started writing poetry as a child and has continued to write for children and adults throughout her life. A first grade teacher for 34 years, Margaret is now retired from teaching and lives in Michigan where she likes to write, take walks in the morning, and care for her three cats.

Photograph by Glenna Washburn

ABOUT THE ADVISER Shannon Cannon contributed the activities pages that appear in this book. Shannon serves as a literacy consultant and provides staff development to help improve reading instruction. She is a frequent presenter at educational conferences and workshops. Prior to this she worked as an elementary school teacher and as president of a curriculum publishing company.